TUESDAY

Found some old letters
Mum wrote to Grandpa
from her travels.
I want to travel too —
like her!!!

Sir David Attenboroughs annual prints

(not grown this year)

please forgive me if I
...
my
...
...the Pope was during
...when all except
1527
...Simon 129, recruited
...of Switzerland.
...in Schurg. — At the
...children
degacends on the
...shepherd to Christ
...Apud, thy lanterns
...Church in October, they
...decorated with blue
... one sent to Curual

Glow in the dark
specimen spores

FRED and the fantastic TUB-TUB

*For Michael Close, who gave
this adventure flight.*

Fred and the Fantastic Tub-Tub
Published in Great Britain in 2022 by Graffeg Limited.

Written by Zeb Soanes copyright © 2022.
Illustrated by Anja Uhren copyright © 2022.
Designed and produced by Graffeg Limited copyright © 2022.

Graffeg Limited, 24 Stradey Park Business Centre, Mwrwg Road,
Llangennech, Llanelli, Carmarthenshire, SA14 8YP, Wales, UK.
Tel: 01554 824000. www.graffeg.com.

The publisher acknowledges the financial support of the
Books Council of Wales. www.gwales.com.

ISBN 9781802580808
eBook ISBN 9781802581317

1 2 3 4 5 6 7 8 9

GRAFFEG

FRED and the fantastic TUB-TUB

by Zeb Soanes

illustrated by Anja Uhren

Also an exciting orchestral concert work

by James Marangone

Introduction

How this adventure took off

In June 2018, I was invited to write a story for an orchestra. The composer James Marangone wanted to create an inclusive narrated adventure that inspired children to explore sound regardless of their musical ability. The suggestion of some sort of flying machine was a playful nod to Michael Close, a retired physics teacher, who generously commissioned the work. It was produced and premiered by the Orpheus Sinfonia, who are passionate about connecting with young audiences. James had already begun experimenting with sound effects from everyday objects and surprising ways of playing traditional instruments – all I had to do was come up with a story...

The environment and our part in its destruction was foremost in the news at the time. The previous November, the BBC broadcast *Blue Planet II*, with harrowing pictures of the damage being done to marine wildlife by discarded plastic. It prompted a remarkable public response to the enormous quantity of unnecessary plastic we produce and throw away every day and in a matter of months plastic drinking straws and cups had all but vanished from cafes and restaurants. In the North Pacific Ocean, the world's plastic pollution collects in what is known as the Great Pacific Garbage Patch – this gave me the idea for the fictional island of Papa Nupi.

Air Mail

I owe the botanical theme to my visits to the Garden Museum at Lambeth, where you can sit in the tranquil restaurant overlooking the tomb of the plant hunter John Tradescant, and the Tub-Tub was inspired by the many exotic plants in the glasshouses at the Royal Botanic Gardens, Kew. Both are well worth a visit.

Writing a story specifically to be set to half an hour of music necessitates the action moving swiftly, so it hasn't been possible to explore the environmental message in great detail, but I hope parents and teachers will make use of the activities at the back of this book to highlight what we can all do to reduce our impact on the planet.

As Grandpa observes, 'With all the troubles in the world, wouldn't it be wonderful if we could all just stop and listen to something beautiful.'

I hope you enjoy reading Fred's adventure and listening to the music it inspired.

London, 2021

Scan the code to listen to the music ↓

graffeg.com/pages/
fred-and-the-fantastic-tub-tub

Fred and the Fantastic Tub-Tub

Fred always looked forward to the summer holiday. Her dad had to work at the hospital, so for six wonderful weeks she got to leave the city and stay with her grandfather in the country. As her train pulled out of the station she could barely contain her excitement. Towers of shiny offices gave way to houses, towns and factories; tiny villages with ancient churches; stately homes with gardens and animals she never saw in the city, like cows and sheep. It was her own special adventure.

Hours later, at the end of the line, the train arrived at a woodland station. Fred was the only person left in the carriage. As she lifted her rucksack, a crumpled face pressed itself against the window. It was Grandpa, grinning mischievously and carrying a bunch of *very unusual* flowers.

Grandpa was a botanist. That means he studied plants. He lived in an untidy farmhouse, surrounded by greenhouses in varying states of disrepair, each home to specimens from different parts of the world. Walking through them was just like being a jungle explorer. Fred's companion on these summer adventures was Sir David Attenborough, Grandpa's cat. Attenborough was sleek and black with yellow eyes. Every mouse and shrew knew to busy themselves elsewhere when he made his morning inspections.

Some greenhouses, like the nursery, were small and plain. Others were glass palaces with ornate domes and finials. They housed plants with beautiful flowers, exotic scents and tall trees that poked through panes, where birds nested in their branches. Attenborough took a dim view of this, but they were too high for him to reach.

Fred rose early to help Grandpa tend his plants and Attenborough went too. Grandpa called her Frederica, which had been her mother's name. Fred chopped off dead flowers with a pair of shears: SNIP – SNAP, SNIP – SNAP – this encouraged more to grow. She sprayed soapy liquid to kill greenfly and a profusion of rainbow bubbles streamed into the air. Attenborough chased them around the greenhouse, then s-t-r-e-t-c-h-e-d out a sharp claw to POP them!

A butterfly flitted above them in the sweet, humid air. Attenborough waited for it to settle, stalked very slowly across the floor, then Pounced! But the butterfly was too quick for him and fluttered by.

For the rest of the day, Fred could do as she pleased. There wasn't another house for miles, so she played with Attenborough. Today they were detectives. She was free to roam wherever she liked, except for one large rusty greenhouse at the end of the farm. The windows had been painted black and a sign on the locked doors read KEEP OUT. Fred imagined whatever plants were inside must be very dangerous. Perhaps they were poisonous – one touch and she'd be dead!? Or carnivorous? Grandpa told her how some plants stank of rotting flesh to lure insects into their bucket-like stomachs, stick to dewey flowers or get snapped between hairy leaves. Or maybe they were like pale deep-sea creatures, able to survive without any light at all? Whatever lived inside was obviously very scary and she had been told she must never EVER go in there.

Each night, after supper, Grandpa answered letters from distant universities, some with unusual seeds taped to them for him to identify, but this night they sat together in the library with their mugs of hot chocolate.

'I have something to show you,' said Grandpa, removing a book from a pouch. 'It's the private notebook of the great plant hunter John Tradescant and my most valuable possession. He travelled all over the world, but there is one place he never got to.' From the book, Grandpa unfolded a fragile map and pointed to a brown blob in the middle. 'The isle of Papa Nupi – so far away few people have ever been there. This map was given to him by someone who had.'

Fred examined it carefully. 'What are those squiggles?' she asked.

'That,' explained Grandpa, 'is the Tub-Tub. Nobody alive has ever seen it. It blooms once every two hundred years. Legend says it produces music so beautiful even the birds in the trees stop singing to hear it.'

Fred thought it sounded fantastic. 'Music,' continued Grandpa, 'is a language everyone can understand. With the many troubles in the world, wouldn't it be wonderful if we could all just stop and listen to something beautiful.' Attenborough stretched and yawned, clearly thinking this was nonsense.

'Cat-nap time,' said Grandpa with a wink. 'Best to bed.'

Fred trudged up the stairs to her little attic room with Attenborough, who curled up on the mattress, purring loudly.

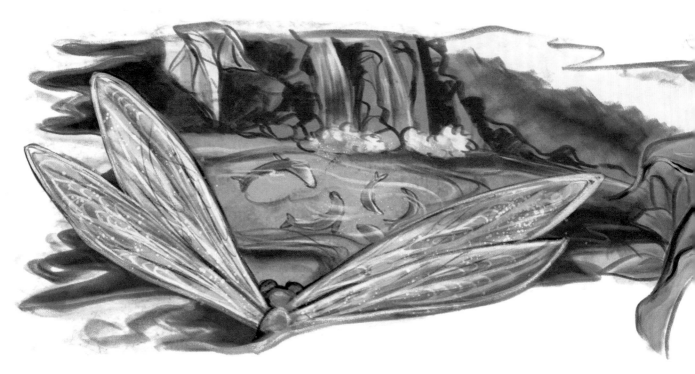

As Fred's eyelids began to close, she imagined what the mysterious island of Papa Nupi might be like...

She was floating over a jungle, the night air cool and sweet. As she glided down through the canopy of branches, the chirruping of crickets made the trees snore. Luminous moths fluttered past a silver waterfall, cascading into a moonlit pool filled with iridescent fish. She gazed at her reflection in the water, but now she was a beautiful damselfly whose silvery wings fizzed when she twitched them. A hungry fish had spied her too and, as she bent to drink, he moved to catch her. Fred darted deep into the jungle, towards the sound of drumming.

Twang! She was caught in a spider's web. Its eight-legged owner scuttled down, plucking the threads like silver strings.

The drums beat louder.

Fred stared into the spider's many eyes as it bound her in silk. She thrashed from side to side, which made the sticky threads grip more tightly until only her head was free.

BANG BANG BANG went the drums.

The spider drew closer, Fred yelled out – and awoke to find herself tangled in her bedsheets. Meanwhile, the BANG BANG BANG was coming from outside the house.

Attenborough, on the window ledge, had heard it too and was staring out across the farmyard. Fred pulled on her dressing gown and they crept downstairs, expecting to hear Grandpa's snoring, but the only sound was the tick, tock of the hallway clock. She strained on tiptoe to listen hard and with a terrific *Riaooooooooow* trod on Attenborough's tail. 'Shhhhhhhh!' whispered Fred. Attenborough looked livid.

They followed the noises out of the back door. The banging had changed to drilling, no, sawing… Sanding? Grinding? Perhaps it was burglars!? The strange sounds grew louder – and were coming from the forbidden greenhouse! A cry rang out that sounded just like Grandpa. What if he was being eaten by one of the carnivorous plants!? Forbidden or not, they had to help him. Fred bounded across the farmyard, leaping over tools, crunching flower pots and nearly tripping over a hosepipe. Attenborough (more carefully) was close behind. The heavy doors to the greenhouse were unlocked and Fred cautiously pushed them open. She couldn't see anything at first; the air was thick with smoke. Then, as it cleared, Fred stood open-mouthed.

Filling the greenhouse was the most incredible contraption. Part of it looked like a boat, and part like a caravan. There was a small greenhouse on the deck. Above, fastened with ropes, was a sausage-shaped balloon and, underneath, dangling by his feet, was Grandpa.

'It was meant to be a surprise!' he cried out feebly.

'But what is it?' Fred asked, helping him down.

'Our transportation!' Grandpa pulled Tradescant's notebook from his pocket and tapped it.

'We're off to Papa Nupi. The last recorded flowering of the Tub-Tub was two hundred years ago next week. We're going to record its remarkable music, so that everyone can hear it!'

'When do we leave?' asked Fred.

'No time like the present,' replied Grandpa. 'I've packed everything, I think...'

Attenborough surveyed his quarters. The flying machine was surprisingly comfortable, with patterned cushions and framed pictures of pressed flowers. The tiny kitchen was stocked with food, including plenty of hot chocolate. Fred thought of her dad back at the hospital. He often worked through the night. He'd love an adventure, she thought, as Grandpa took leather straps from under the cushions and fastened her in.

'How will we get out of the greenhouse?' she enquired, looking around them.

'Through the roof, of course!' chirped Grandpa, and he pulled a lever.

There was an almighty clanking as chains turned rusty cogs and the roof of the greenhouse slowly creaked open. Panes of glass crashed to the floor and birds flew up to the sky. Grandpa heaved heavy sacks off the deck and the flying machine began to strain. It bashed this way and that as it started to rise, rattling and clattering the crockery in the kitchen.

'Will it fit through the roof?' Fred asked, nervously.

'Hopefully...' replied Grandpa. 'Hold on tight!' he called, throwing over the last sack. 'We're off!' The flying machine squeezed its way out like a loaf of bread rising from a tin.

'It's going to BURST!' cried Fred, covering her ears. And then, with an almighty FLUMP, they rose swiftly and gracefully up, up, up into the air.

Beneath them the farm grew smaller and smaller. Grandpa turned on the engines and the flying machine sailed across the early morning sky. Sheep scattered fields, wild horses galloped over moorland and a flock of noisy seagulls led them far out over the sea.

The flying machine creaked like a galleon, far above the boats below and low enough to go unnoticed by planes overhead. Fred's phone pinged with a message from her dad asking, *'How's your holiday?'*

'Oh fine,' she replied breezily. 'Grandpa's taking me birdwatching!'

'You young people are always on your phones,' Grandpa complained gently. He didn't even have an email address and preferred to write all his letters by hand.

By day Grandpa steered the ship using his enormous compass. Fred wondered why he didn't just follow the map on her phone – but he liked to do things the old way, and it made him happy.

There were many useful modern landmarks, like oil rigs, not featured on Tradescant's map, and it cautioned of ancient dangers, like sea monsters, which Grandpa explained were simply whales. A humpback soared out of the sea beneath them and smashed back into the ocean with a mighty splash.

At night they sat on deck with their hot chocolate, gazing at stars and learning all about Papa Nupi from the notebook. The island was uninhabited until a ship was wrecked off its coastline hundreds of years ago. Its crew were the first to hear the Tub-Tub's music and have stayed to protect it ever since.

'I wonder if they have cats?' said Fred, looking at Attenborough, who was pawing at a moth fluttering around the reading lamp.

The air grew suddenly cold, there was a damp smell, the sky flashed and rain lashed upon them. 'Inside!' shouted Grandpa.

Attenborough bounded for cover and Fred grabbed the notebook. Buffeted by terrific winds, the flying machine lurched up and down. Grandpa held tight, trying to steer them through the storm. There was an almighty...

CRACK

Fred felt her stomach heave into her chest.

They were falling!

Faster and faster.

Grandpa appeared at the door with a crazed look.

'Grab cushions!'

he yelled.

'It's going to be a bumpy landing!'

23

When they opened their eyes they were in darkness. Outside: the sound of lapping water. Fred wondered if sea monsters existed after all and they had been swallowed by one. Just then, they heard something.

'Pa-pa Nu-pi, Pa-pa Nu-pi, Pa-pa Nu-pi, Pa-pa Nu-pi!'

It sounded like singing.

'Pa-pa Nu-pi, Pa-pa Nu-pi, Pa-pa Nu-pi, Pa-pa Nu-pi!'

It was getting closer.

In a flash, they were dazzled by light. As their eyes adjusted, they saw they were surrounded by the smiling islanders of Papa Nupi on dozens of little boats. The flying machine had landed on the sea, covered with the empty balloon, which the islanders rolled up onto a raft. Ropes were attached to the flying machine and Fred, Grandpa and Attenborough were gently towed to shore.

To Fred the island didn't look real, like one of the gardens-in-a-bottle Grandpa had on the windowsills at home. There were tall purple mountains with birds circling overhead, a waterfall cascading through lush green jungle to a white beach that shimmered brightly in the sunlight like diamonds.

The Papa Nupians hauled the flying machine onto the shore, next to the wreck of the *Theophrastus*, the ship that had delivered their ancestors. From the deck they were greeted by the island's captain, who wore a flamboyant hat made from washing-up bottles. 'I am Captain Kosmos,' he announced.

'Pleased to meet you, captain,' replied Grandpa. 'I'm Arthur Merriweather.'
They shook hands and the islanders repeated this new name with curiosity.

'Merri-weather, Merri-weather, Merri-weather, Merri-weather.'

The Papa Nupians wore extremely unusual clothes, all made from bits of coloured plastic. In fact, the beach was not sand or shimmering jewels as Fred had first thought but millions of pieces of washed-up plastic that the islanders used for everything. Fred took a picture for her dad.

'You are welcome!' proclaimed the captain. 'We are preparing for a special celebration – and must drink schmoo!'

'Schmoo?' repeated Grandpa.

A wooden barrel was produced, into which the captain dunked an arm and removed a leaky leather boot, overflowing with brownish liquid. Fred pulled a face and was handed a coconut and straw from the beach. 'Doesn't he mean shoe?' she whispered. Not wishing to offend, Grandpa tasted the liquid... and then again, more enthusiastically.

'No, Frederica, schmoo will do!' The islanders cheered.

Feeling very warmly welcome, Grandpa announced, 'We have come to hear the Tub-Tub.' The cheering turned to chanting:

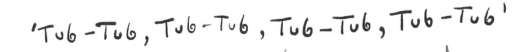

'Tub-Tub, Tub-Tub, Tub-Tub, Tub-Tub'

Captain Kosmos stepped forward with an accusing look.

'You have come to **STEAL** the Tub-Tub?'

'No, really!' assured Grandpa, hastily reaching for his notebook. 'I merely want to *record it*.'

Grandpa invited the captain aboard the flying machine and demonstrated his phonograph, an antique device that recorded sound onto wax cylinders. Grandpa put on his poetry hat with the little tassel, and, turning the wheel of his machine, recited his favourite verse to demonstrate:

'In days of old,
When knights were bold
 and dragons bothered kings,
 A boy named George,
  rode forth with sword
  to slay the fiery things.
  The king had promised George his daughter,
  if the fearsome beast he'd slaughter,
  But George being kind,
  he changed his mind
and quenched the dragon's fire with water!'

Captain Kosmos laughed and slapped his thigh. Grandpa wound the wax cylinder back to the beginning and played his recording. The captain leapt to his feet, called for more schmoo and, in turn, recorded a *rather rude* song (which I'm not allowed to repeat).

That evening they marched to the glade where the Tub-Tub grew. Along the way they made music from things that they found: tambourines from the lids of coffee cups, plastic-tubing trumpets and water-cooler-bottle drums.

The islanders had been preparing for this night for many years, but as fast as they tried to clear the jungle of rubbish, reusing it however they could, more washed up on the beach. The wildlife also had no choice but to live with it and nests in the trees resembled woven baskets of coloured net and rope.

'The world's sea currents must bring it *here*,' observed Grandpa, looking to the horizon, where more plastic was on its way.

'There'll soon be no room for the Tub-Tub,' remarked the captain, and Fred held back to take a picture.

After an hour, they reached the heart of the jungle. No living soul had seen the Tub-Tub, yet all around them tall stones marked the spot, etched from ages past. The carvings looked more like a machine than a plant. Captain Kosmos and Grandpa talked animatedly, gazing into the sky, and Fred was amazed they could tell it was time for the Tub-Tub from only the position of the stars.

They cleared the ground of rubbish, then settled themselves and waited: feasting, dancing and sleeping in the glade, until quite suddenly the earth beneath them rumbled. Monkeys shrieked high in the trees. Birds squawked overhead and in the faraway mountains unknown beasts roared. 'Tub-Tub, Tub-Tub,' whispered the islanders. Then, just as Grandpa had read, every creature fell silent. He started to wind the phonograph... and it began. With a terrific creaking, hollow stalks shot from the ground like organ pipes, a cascade of bell flowers bloomed at the top and enormous leaves unfurled like ears to catch the breeze. The sun had nearly set and, as the cool night wind began to whisper through the trees and into the Tub-Tub's elephantine leaves, a low sound shook the earth. The sound swirled around them and, as it rose above the trees, it lifted their cares with it. There was no feeling of the past or the future, everyone felt completely content.

The sound filled their hearts with such joy that with one voice everyone began to sing. They sang with all their hearts until the sun began to rise. The Tub-Tub folded over, exhaling with a heavy sigh, and by morning was only a hush of leaves upon the jungle floor. Everyone had been changed by the beauty of the night before. They couldn't explain it, but they felt it.

Captain Kosmos stood before them. 'You have heard the ancient song of the Tub-Tub. We will not live to hear it again, *but* with your wonderful talking machine we can hear it always. Leave it with us and go in peace.'

'Leave it!?' exclaimed Grandpa. 'But it's the reason we came, so the world can hear it!'

The captain looked grave. '*It* stays on Papa Nupi or *you* stay on Papa Nupi.'

Fred whispered, 'But Grandpa... you *can* leave your machine.' Grandpa stared in disbelief, then saw what she was waving in her hand.

'I recorded the whole thing on my phone,' she explained. 'I even took a video for Dad.' Grandpa's face burst into a broad smile, then he turned to the captain.

'We have been privileged to share an occasion none of us will ever forget. I will leave my talking machine and, thanks to my clever granddaughter, we will do all in our power to stop Papa Nupi becoming the world's rubbish dump.' The captain embraced him warmly. 'In return,' added Grandpa, 'I wonder if I might have your recipe for schmoo?' The islanders cheered. 'Come on, Frederica,' said Grandpa, taking her hand, 'we're going home.'

That afternoon the Papa Nupians carried the flying machine to the highest cliff on the island. They patched up the balloon with carrier bags, lit a fire and filled it with hot air from an enormous pair of bellows, which made a rude noise that made them all giggle.

On board, Attenborough came to greet them. He had spent all this time eating fish and sunbathing. They were handed baskets of food for the journey and he looked to see if there was any more for him.

Grandpa and Fred thanked the captain, who tucked the schmoo recipe into Grandpa's jacket. The islanders unlashed ropes and gently pushed the flying machine off the cliff. Its engines whirred and with one last look back and a wave goodbye they flew out over the great wide sea towards home.

'Look after that phone of yours,' Grandpa cautioned. 'That recording will be the greatest botanical discovery in history. I'll have to think of a better name than Tub-Tub, though.'

'It was like a great peace organ,' said Fred, who was busy texting.

'*Pacem Organum* Tub-Tub,' pondered Grandpa. 'I rather like that!'

Fred's phone started pinging furiously. 'Someone's popular,' sighed Grandpa.

'It's us!' exclaimed Fred. 'We've gone viral!' Fred had sent her photos and the recording of the Tub-Tub to one or two of her schoolfriends, who shared it with three or more of their friends. Someone posted it on the internet and by the time Grandpa and Fred arrived home the wondrous music of the Tub-Tub had spread all around the world. Everyone was horrified to see how their toothpaste caps and water bottles had very nearly destroyed such an extraordinary place and, moved by the Tub-Tub's powerful music, all the governments decided to have a very serious meeting about it. Fred, Grandpa and Attenborough were famous. And, because music is a language everyone can understand, *this* is how their story is told.

Zeb Soanes
- author -

Zeb Soanes is an author, broadcaster and concert narrator. He studied Drama and Creative Writing at UEA and created the bestselling *Gaspard the Fox* series of books, illustrated by James Mayhew, inspired by his remarkable encounters with a real urban fox. He is a newsreader and reassuring voice of the Shipping Forecast to millions of listeners on BBC Radio 4 and launched the television channel BBC Four, where he presented the BBC Proms. He performs favourite concert works for children with the UK's leading orchestras and is a patron of Awards for Young Musicians, supporting talented children from low-income families to pursue their musical ambitions.

Anja Uhren
- illustrator -

Anja Uhren is a Sheffield-based illustrator and storyteller, working with images and words to deliver emotionally driven narratives. Her work focuses on the small moments – the magic and beauty of everyday life, observations and encounters. Originally from Germany, Anja moved to the UK to study illustration and has been self-employed in the creative industry ever since graduating from the Arts University Bournemouth. She has recently become a new mum and rediscovering the world through her son's eyes gives her plenty of inspiration for her work. Gardening and journaling are also some of her favourite things, which has made this project such a pleasure to illustrate.

FUN FACTS

- The shipwreck of the *Theophrastus* is named after the Greek philosopher, widely considered to be the father of botany. He created the first classification of plants, dividing them into four broad categories: herbs, trees, shrubs and subshrubs. His *Enquiry into Plants* is regarded as one of the most important books of ancient times.

- Captain *Kosmos* is named after the title of a book by the great scientist-explorer and plant-hunter Alexander Von Humbolt. He believed that everything in nature was interconnected – a new way of thinking – and, in 1799, was the first person to link climate change to human activity.

- *Papa Nupi* is an imaginary island but the name was based on Rapa Nui, more commonly known as Easter Island, famous for its nearly 1,000 giant stone statues.

- Grandpa's talking machine, the *phonograph*, invented by Thomas Edison in 1887, was the earliest practical method of recording and playing back sound. You spoke into a horn which caused a needle to vibrate on a rotating foil or wax cylinder. When you wound the cylinder back, it played what you had recorded. This hand-operated machine led to the development of all recorded music.

- Grandpa's cat is named after the broadcaster and naturalist Sir David Attenborough, who powerfully raised awareness of the plastic crisis in our oceans through his series *Blue Planet II*.

- The *Tub-Tub* is a fantasy creation but in my mind was inspired by several different plants which you can find pictures of online:

Gunnera
(also called giant rhubarb)

Pitcher plant

Organ pipe cactus

make a Green Wall

& watch your seeds grow

(you might even grow a Tub-Tub)

How you can reduce plastic waste ↓

- Say 'no' to plastic straws, use paper or reusable metal or bamboo ones instead.
- Avoid snacks in plastic packaging.
- Don't buy water in plastic bottles, carry a reusable bottle instead.
- Buy individual fruit and vegetables that aren't wrapped in plastic.
- Avoid plastic carrier bags. Keep a reusable bag for when you go to the shops.
- Sometimes we have to use plastic, but always try to reuse it and never drop it as litter where it can blow away and become a problem for wildlife. If we can all make small changes to the way we live and shop, the benefit to the planet will be enormous.

45

Start your own
Journal here

then continue in your book of choice

Collect

- scraps of paper & other flat material
- photographs
- to-do lists
- diary entries
- doodles
- dried flowers

and more

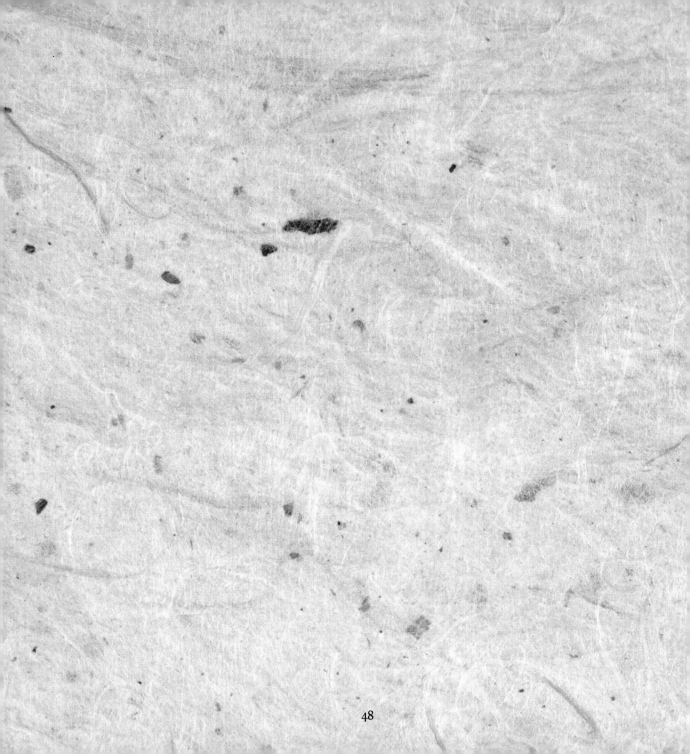

PAPA NUPI adventur

Me & Captain

Plastic waste

Samples

more photos

Schmoo recipe

We saw the most magnificent PLANTS & Beasts

No more fruits in nets!

TOP SECRET

CONFIDENTIAL